GASTON
The Green~Nosed Alligator
COLORING BOOK

Written and Illustrated by
JAMES RICE

The Illustrator of
CAJUN NIGHT BEFORE CHRISTMAS

PELICAN PUBLISHING COMPANY
GRETNA 1998

First printing, 1976
Second printing, 1994
Third printing, 1998

Printed in India

Published by Pelican Publishing Company, Inc.
P.O. Box 3110, Gretna, Louisiana 70054-3110

Quaint old Santa Claus
in his house made of ice.

The reindeer were shirking
and working too slow.

His reindeer had stayed
at the North Pole alone.

The reindeer last Christmas
had nearly run late.

Santa poled down the bayou
and let his thoughts roam.

The problem's solution
he'd find near this home.

A great fireplace blazing
and workshop well fit.

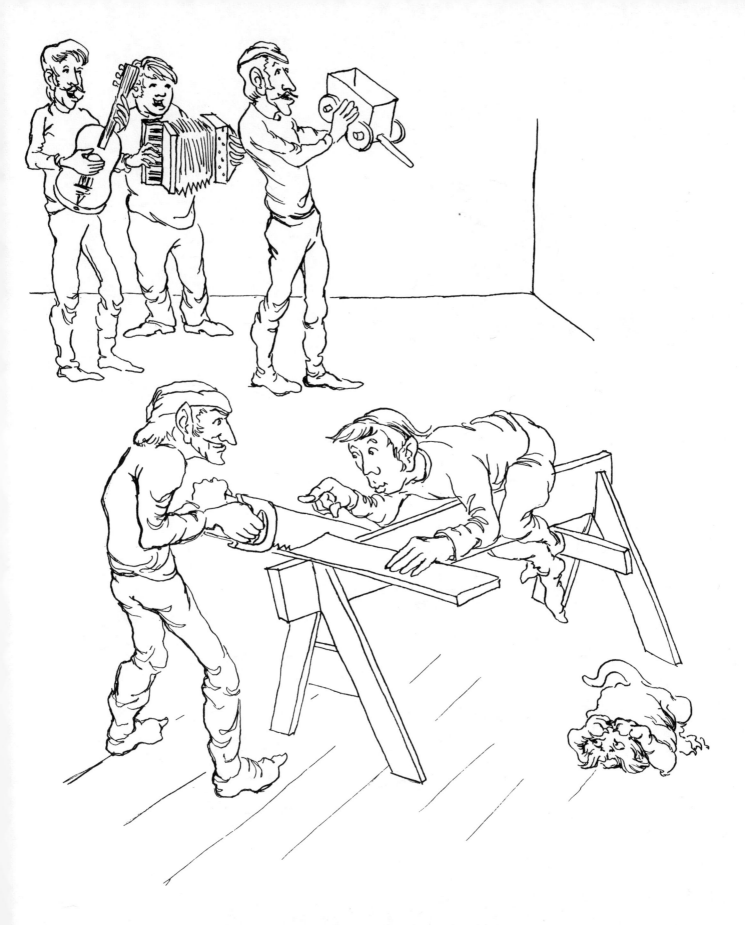

With sawing and hammering
and busy elves singing.

With tools and work tables
for building of toys.

Old Santa was worried

From out of the corner
of his left eye he spied

Swooping and gliding
  through the tops of the trees.

While ol' Gaston flew
he put on a show

While most of the alligators
swam muddy and slimy.

His problem was solved,
  no more reindeer he'd need.

"Stop, you strange creature,
and come here to me!"

But they'd crash into trees
and fall on their tails,

They'd try it again
and still they would fail.

But they wouldn't give up
'till they'd mastered the skill.

Now practice was over,
   it was near time to leave.

They loaded the gift bags

In the skiff up so high,

Full of toys and goodies
and every good gift.

Ol' Gaston would help,
there was no need to plead.

They didn't miss a stop
    on their fantastic flight.

A sleepy old Cajun
   looked up with a yawn,

A little old man
with an outlandish team

With a wave of his hand
and an echo so slight.

"MERRY CHRISTMAS TO ALL
'TILL I SAW YA SOME MO'!"